Secrets! DAViD MORTiMORE BAXTER

by Karen Tayleur

illustrated by Brann Garvey

CONTRA COSTA COUNTY LIBRARY

Librarian Reviewer
Kathleen Baxter
Children's Literature Consultant
formerly with Anoka County Library, MN
BA College of Saint Catherine, St. Paul, MN
MA in Library Science, University of Minnesota

Reading Consultant
Elizabeth Stedem
Educator/Consultant, Colorado Springs, CO
MA in Elementary Education, University of Denver, CO

WITHDRAWN

STONE ARCH BOOKS
Minneapolis   San Diego

3 1901 04146 2518

First published in the United States in 2007
by Stone Arch Books,
151 Good Counsel Drive, P.O. Box 669,
Mankato, Minnesota 56002.
www.stonearchbooks.com

Published by arrangement with Black Dog Books.

Text copyright © 2004 Karen Tayleur

All rights reserved. No part of this publication may be reproduced
in whole or in part, or stored in a retrieval system, or transmitted in any
form or by any means, electronic, mechanical, photocopying, recording,
or otherwise, without written permission of the publisher.

Library of Congress Cataloging-in-Publication Data
Tayleur, Karen.
    Secrets!: The Secret Life of David Mortimore Baxter / by Karen Tayleur;
illustrated by Brann Garvey.
    p. cm. — (David Mortimore Baxter)
    Summary: When professional wrestler Smashing Smorgan tells the world that
young David Mortimore Baxter is good at keeping secrets, everyone from odd neighbor
McCafferty to school bully Victor Sneddon loads David up with more secrets than he
can handle.
    ISBN-13: 978-1-59889-077-8 (hardcover)
    ISBN-10: 1-59889-077-8 (hardcover)
    ISBN-13: 978-1-59889-209-3 (paperback)
    ISBN-10: 1-59889-209-6 (paperback)
    [1. Secrets—Fiction. 2. Humorous stories.] I. Garvey, Brann, ill. II. Title. III.
Title: Secret Life of David Mortimore Baxter. IV. Series: Tayleur, Karen. David
Mortimore Baxter.
PZ7.T21149Se 2007
[Fic]—dc22   2006005077

Art Director: Heather Kindseth
Graphic Designer: Kay Fraser

Photo Credits
Delaney Photography, cover

1   2   3   4   5   6   11   10   09   08   07   06

Printed in the United States of America

Table of Contents

My friend **Smashing Smorgan** is a famous wrestler. Sometimes it's good to know a star like Smorgan. But sometimes it's bad.

Once Smorgan gave me tickets for the World Wrestling Mania finals. He also gave me a pass to the party afterward. I got to meet all my favorite wrestlers. That's when it's good to know someone famous.

Then there was the time Smashing Smorgan told me a really important secret. That was a bad time to have smorgan as a friend.

I didn't ask him to tell me. It's not like I said, "Smorgan, is there anything secret you want to tell me?" I was minding my own business. But one day Smorgan called to share some news with me.

"Davey, I've got some **great news**. It's going to blow this town away. And I want you to be the first to know."

"Oh. **Okay**," I said.

Smorgan told me that at the Wrestling Mania Awards, he was going to be inducted into the Hall of Fame.

"Great!" I said. "What does inducted mean?"

"It means that my name's going to be added to a whole list of famous wrestlers in the history books. And I get a gold trophy. And my photo will be in the Wrestling Hall of Fame forever!"

"Until the end of the world?" I asked.

"Yep," said Smorgan.

"Until the end of the universe?" I asked.

"Yep," said Smorgan.

"COOL," I said.

"It's a secret until the awards night. You can't tell anyone, okay?" Smorgan said.

"Sure," I said.

* * *

I forgot all about Smorgan's secret until the night of the Wrestling Mania Awards.

Me and Dad and Harry and Boris were all watching TV. Harry was trying to get Boris to **beg for chips,** but Boris was too busy sleeping.

"And the wrestler inducted into the Hall of Fame this year . . ." said the announcer.

"Oh," I said, remembering Smorgan's secret.

" . . . **is Smashing Smorgan!**"

The crowd went wild. Dad and Harry **hooted** and **cheered.** Even Boris **opened one eye.**

The camera picked Smorgan out of the audience. **He was trying to look surprised.** Then he shook his head as if he couldn't believe it. He stood up. The cheering got **L͎O͎U͎D͎E͎R͎** as he made his way to the microphone.

When the crowd calmed down, Smorgan **wiped a tear from his cheek.** The presenter handed the award to Smorgan and slapped him on the shoulder.

Smorgan made a nice speech. He thanked **his best rivals,** Mad Dog Matty and Sick Freddy Smith.

Then his manager, Ivan (who was retiring after twenty years). Then the guy who made his **silver platform boots**. Finally, he thanked his mother.

The announcer moved forward to the microphone and said, "You can't tell me this is a surprise, Smorgan. You've known about this award for some time."

Smorgan grinned. "You're right, Bert. And there's one more person I need to thank."

He looked straight into the camera. It felt like he was looking **right at me**.

"There's a boy out there — you know who you are, David Mortimore Baxter — who managed to keep this **secret** for the past month. Good job, Davey. You're a **good friend!**"

The crowd **went wild again**. Smorgan held up his trophy and the screen cut to a commercial. Dad leaned over and punched me lightly on the arm. He had a really weird look on his face.

"**David, good job**," he mumbled. I thought he might cry.

"Well, **yeah**," I said.

Harry's **JAW** had **dropped** and his eyes were wide.

"**What?**" I demanded.

"I am the brother of someone who has been mentioned on national television by **Smashing Smorgan**," he said. "**I am famous**." Then he ran out of the room yelling for Mom.

Then the phone started ringing. First **JOE** called. He is my **best friend** and a movie nut. Joe said he had it all on videotape if I wanted a copy.

Then **Bec** called to ask why I hadn't told her Smorgan's secret. **What kind of friend was I?** (Bec is **my other best friend**. You can have two, you know.) Then Bec put Ralph on the phone. Ralph wouldn't talk to me. That's okay, since Ralph is Bec's pet rat. Ralph and Bec and Joe and I all belong to a **secret club**. It's called the Secret Club, because we haven't figured out a name for it yet.

Then Mr. **McCafferty**, our neighbor, called. He said he'd just turned his television on and heard my name. **He wanted to know if I'd finally ended up in jail.**

Then Gran called and wanted to know *when I'd become a wrestler.* And wasn't I too young? And shouldn't I finish school before I decided on a career? (I didn't get a chance to ask why she was watching wrestling awards.)

Then some reporter called asking if this was the home of David Mortimore Baxter. *I told her no.*

Then Rose Thornton called. Mom says I'm not allowed to hate people, so *I really, really, really don't like Rose Thornton.*

"Baxter, do you know that your phone is broken? I haven't been able to get through for the past two hours," she said.

"Actually, it is working. I've been using it," I said. "Why were you calling?"

"I just wanted to tell you that your phone was broken. Good night," she said. Then she slammed the phone down.

Mom unplugged the phone from the wall. "This is ridiculous," she said. "No more calls tonight."

I walked into the living room. My sister, Zoe, had actually left her room for once. She asked if any of the calls had been for her.

"Nope," I said. "Zoe, **what's the big deal?** Someone mentions my name on TV and suddenly everyone wants to talk to me."

"That was your fifteen minutes of fame, little brother," said Zoe. She was sitting in an armchair looking bored, but I could tell she was IMPRESSED.

"Fame? As in famous? Why fifteen minutes? Why not five or twenty?" I asked.

"**Dribbles**, it's a saying. Some guy once said We all get fifteen minutes of fame in our life. Looks like yours came early."

"Oh. Okay," I said. I was glad my fifteen minutes were over with and I could get on with the rest of my life.

Unfortunately my fame lasted **a lot** longer than fifteen minutes.

CHAPTER 2

THE JOKE

At school the next day, all the kids in my class crowded around **Ms. Stacey's** desk. Someone was making fake kissing noises. I pushed past Jake and ducked under the arms of the GG's, Rose's Giggling Girls, to get a look.

One of the girls noticed me. "Well, look who it is. **Mr. Famous.**"

I ignored her.

There, on Ms. Stacey's computer, was the **ugliest picture** I'd ever seen. A monster's face. A sharp crooked nose ended in two huge black caves. Thick black hairs stuck out of each nostril. Little red lines swam across the whites of both eyes. Huge ears looked like something you could climb.

It was **Smorgan**. Everybody knew that Ms. Stacey had a crush on Smashing Smorgan, but we didn't talk about it. It was supposed to be a secret. Who would do that to Ms. Stacey?

"That's disgusting," said Joe. He sniffed. He had a cold. Suddenly all the kids made their way back to their desks. I was standing at Ms. Stacey's desk when she came in. She threw down her books, looked at the monitor, and **stared**. Someone coughed. I think it was Joe.

"Ms. Stacey?" I said.

She kept staring without a word. She looked like she'd just seen my bedroom before I cleaned it up. Then she turned and walked **out** of the class. I noticed her hands were SHAKING. I looked at Bec.

"Go find her," Bec whispered.

I could think of a thousand reasons why I shouldn't.

I left the room. First I checked the teachers' lounge and found Ms. Stacey. Then I thought I'd get Ms. Lutsky, the office lady, but Ms. Stacey grabbed my arm.

"I can't, I can't," she said. Her hands were still shaking.

"I don't know how that picture got there," I said.

I found a pack of hot cocoa mix and microwaved some water.

"It was probably a computer virus or something," I said.

I added some milk and sugar to the water and cocoa. Then I added a spoon of coffee in case she wanted coffee. Then I added **more** sugar. **I figured it couldn't hurt.**

"Maybe Ms. Lutsky can fix it. She's pretty good at computer stuff," I said.

By the time I carried the cup over to her, I'd **spilled** half of it. Ms. Stacey grabbed the cup and **spilled the rest** of it onto the table. Then our art teacher, Mrs. George, came in. She told me to go back to class.

Back in class, Principal Woods was writing on the board. "**Sit down, David**, and answer these questions from the board," he said, not turning around.

I looked around the class, searching for the guilty person.

Jake was GOOFY, but I couldn't imagine him doing something like that.

He probably didn't even know how to change the computer's display.

Rose was busy writing. Her cheeks were red and giving off enough heat to toast a marshmallow. She could have been feeling guilty, or just embarrassed.

Bec was **chewing** the end of her pen and looking at the board. She had no reason to pick on Ms. Stacey.

Joe was sniffing loudly next to me. When I looked at him, he **wiped his nose on his sleeve.**

I looked over the rest of the class. It was crazy, but as mean as Ms. Stacey could get, **no one would want to hurt her.** She was okay, for a teacher. I really couldn't think of anyone who would do something like that to her. The room was quiet except for the scratching of pens on paper and Joe's sniffing.

Bec raised her hand.

"Yes, Rebecca," said Mr. Woods. He didn't turn around. He must have eyes in the back of his head like my mom.

"We're supposed to be working in the art room on our **Bays Park Fair project**," said Bec.

"Until someone admits to touching Ms. Stacey's computer, we will stay here. You will answer these questions from the board. And you will do it quietly," he added, as a buzz of whispering went around the room.

I wondered if I'd be home in time for dinner. Or my eighteenth birthday. Maybe I'd never get my driver's license. Maybe I'd grow old and die here. Mom would be really mad if I wasn't home for the rest of my life.

The bell rang for recess. A few kids looked up and moved around in their seats. But Mr. Woods kept writing.

It was going to be a **long day**.

CHAPTER 3

SECRETS

Mr. Woods finally let us out at lunchtime. Me and Bec and Joe got together under the oak tree. I suggested that the **Secret Club Spy Agency** might be able to track down the computer villain.

"The Secret Club Spy Agency?" repeated Bec. "Since when have we had an agency?"

SPYING was one of the Secret Club's favorite ways to spend time. We hid behind trees. Put clues together. Sometimes we spied on each other. The first person to creep up on the other two players was the winner. This was called MSV. That meant Maximum Surprise Value.

"Just an idea," I began.

"I think someone wants to talk to you," interrupted Joe.

Jake Davern was standing near us. "**Pssst,**" he hissed. "**Pssssssssst.**"

I pointed to my chest and he nodded. I walked over.

It turned out that Jake wanted to tell me a secret. He'd been dying to tell someone, but there wasn't anyone he could trust **until now**.

"I saw the Wrestling Awards last night," he explained.

I nodded.

"So I can trust you, right?"

I **shrugged**.

"I did something dumb the other day," he said.

Wow, what a surprise, I thought. "Did you touch Ms. Stacey's computer?" I asked.

"No. Not that. It was the other day. In story writing class. When we were on the computers. I kind of deleted Kaya's story. The one she wrote for the contest."

"And she didn't get her story into the contest because someone deleted it," I said.

"Yeah. I didn't do it on purpose. **I didn't know she was using the dumb computer**. Ms. Stacey told us we had to go back to class. I didn't see any story. I just turned it off."

"So what are you going to do?" I asked.

"Nothing." Jake grinned. "I just needed to tell someone. I feel better now. Remember, **it's a secret**. See you later." Jake ran off, making his **monkey noises**. That's when a GIRL appeared from out of nowhere.

"Hi, David," she said.

"Hi," I said.

"I just need to tell you something," she said.

Oh no!

"You know your friend Joe?"

"I guess if he's my friend, I must know him," I said. I could feel my ears getting hot. When I talked to strange girls, my ears always did that.

"Yeah, well, Kaya thinks Joe is really cool." The girl **giggled**. "You're not allowed to tell anyone," she said, before she ran off.

I didn't believe her. **How could Kaya think Joe was cool?**

That's when I saw **Victor Sneddon**, the school bully, marching right up to me. His face was bent into a huge frown. I thought about running, but I knew that he'd just catch up with me.

I decided to face him.

"**What's up, Victor?**" I said, in my best wrestler's voice. It sounded deep and growly in my head, but it came out high and squeaky.

"I hear there was **some trouble** this morning," he said.

I nodded.

"Well? **Tell me**," he demanded.

I explained to Victor about the screensaver. I told him about Ms. Stacey getting upset and Mr. Woods taking over our class.

"That's too bad," he said. "How upset was Ms. Stacey?"

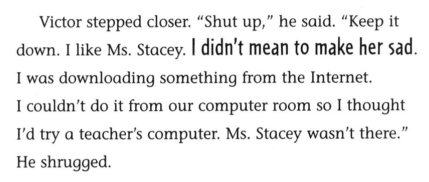

"Really upset," I said.

"Did she cry?" he asked.

"What do you care?" I asked. "Unless you did it!"

Victor stepped closer. "Shut up," he said. "Keep it down. I like Ms. Stacey. I didn't mean to make her sad. I was downloading something from the Internet. I couldn't do it from our computer room so I thought I'd try a teacher's computer. Ms. Stacey wasn't there." He shrugged.

"You downloaded a picture of **Smashing Smorgan**?" I asked.

"I was going to save it on a disk. But then I heard someone coming. So I left."

"Now we're all in trouble because of you. Ms. Stacey thought someone was playing a trick on her. So what are you going to do about it?"

"Nothing," said Victor. "And neither are you. No one needs to know. And you're not going to tell them."

I looked up, and up, until I reached Victor's face. His head was blocking out the sun.

"Okay," I said. I didn't have a death wish. Having Mr. Woods as a teacher was nothing compared to being on Victor Sneddon's bad side.

Mr. Woods was our teacher for the rest of the day. There was a rumor going around that Ms. Stacey had been taken away in an ambulance. Someone said that she'd gone CRAZY and deleted all our permanent records from the computer. Someone else said that the police were going to interview us.

Before we left, Mr. Woods gave us a **huge amount of homework** to do. When the final bell rang, I couldn't wait to get out of there.

CHAPTER 4

BUSTED BIG TIME!

When I got home, I decided to do my homework right away. But I needed tape, and the tape dispenser was empty. I tracked down Harry. **Harry** loves sticky tape. This time he'd used it all to make a mummy for his Halloween model. Even after I yelled at him for using the tape, he kept smiling.

"What are you smiling at?" I asked.

"Today I got three new baseball cards, a pack of gum, and a doughnut for free. Just because I'm your brother."

Harry was the most popular kid in his class, since Smorgan said my name on TV. Nothing would put Harry in a **bad mood**.

I checked in the kitchen drawers for some tape. Nothing. I checked the hallway drawers. I found tablecloths, old batteries, and one shoelace, but no tape.

That's when I noticed that Zoe's bedroom door was open.

Zoe never left her door open. Maybe she was lying on the floor dead! Maybe she'd been kidnapped and there was a ransom note! Maybe she'd stopped being a teenager and had turned into a NORMAL person again!

I looked in her room, but it was empty. While I was there, I decided I'd look for some tape. Okay, maybe I was just snooping.

I checked her wardrobe. All her clothes were organized by color. They were all **black**.

I checked under her bed. I checked under the mattress of her bed.

I found her diary in the third drawer of her bedside table. I knew it was Zoe's diary, because Gran had given the same one to me and Harry and Zoe for Christmas last year.

I looked at the diary. There was no lock on it, but I couldn't just open it. I mean, a diary's personal, **right?** But it might happen to fall open!

I dropped the diary on her bed and it fell open to the bookmarked section.

"I love him. If our parents don't agree, we'll just have to run away and get married. It's the only . . ."

"Who said you could come in here?"

I swung around. Zoe had her hands on her hips.

"I didn't mean to," I began. I closed the diary and put it back in the drawer.

"Shut up," said Zoe. "How much did you read?"

"Enough," I said.

"Well, now you know. What are you going to do about it?"

I wasn't sure what to say. "Zoe, you've got to talk to Mom and Dad."

"No, David. I need to work this out for myself. Maybe I'll tell them later," she said.

"But later's too late!"

Zoe grabbed me by the shoulders. "Listen, you!"

Mom passed Zoe's bedroom doorway. Zoe hugged me with one arm. Mom backtracked to see what was going on.

"Everything all right in here?" asked Mom.

Zoe laughed. "This kid!" she said, giving me a squeeze. "Don't you just love him?" She SQUEEZED me harder.

"You're hurting me," I muttered.

"Keep smiling," Zoe muttered back.

Mom left, shaking her head. Zoe closed the door behind her.

"This is my secret. You kept Smorgan's secret. You have to keep quiet until I figure out what to do. Or else. Promise?" she said.

I nodded. We spit into each other's palms and slapped a high five.

"You'd better tell them soon," I said. "They might want to be there."

Zoe ruffled my hair. "Maybe, Dribbles. Now get."

I grabbed Boris's leash and took him for a walk. I thought it might clear my head, but I just took my trouble with me. My sister was running away to get married. Zoe had lots of friends, but I didn't know she had a **boyfriend**. Mom and Dad would kill her.

A shadow fell on the path in front of me.

"What's up, David?"

It was **Bec**. She had Ralph on a leash. He was busy exploring the trash collected around the light pole.

"Bec! What are you doing here?"

Bec pointed to the nearest building. "I live here," she said.

I hadn't realized where I was walking.

"You look kind of strange," said Bec.

I shrugged.

"Do you want to talk about it?" asked Bec.

"I can't," I said. "It's a SECRET."

Bec patted Boris. "Joe and I were going to come over for a game of Spies," said Bec. "It was such a bad day."

"Not today. I've got homework to do," I said sadly.

I turned around and walked back home. I wondered if Zoe had run away yet.

The only thing that could make this day any **worse** would be **vegetarian loaf** for dinner.

CHAPTER 5

TROUBLE

When I got home, Mom told me she made veggie loaf for dinner. Just the smell of it cooking made my **stomach** want to **hide**. I looked in the fridge for something else to eat. Mom was on me like mold on an old sandwich.

"No eating before dinner," she said. "You don't want to SPOIL your appetite."

Actually, that was **exactly** what I wanted to do. I watched her pull the vegetarian loaf out of the oven. The cheese on top was still bubbling.

"Hot dish coming through," she sang out as she walked to the dining room. "Davey, put that dog outside, please." Mom placed the dish carefully on the small table near the dining room window.

I wondered if Harry had any food hidden in his room. There was nothing in Harry's room or mine. Zoe's room was locked. There was no answer when I knocked. In the study I found **Dad** munching on potato chips. He offered me the bag.

"Vegetarian loaf for dinner," he said with a **frown**.

I grabbed a handful of chips and went back to the kitchen for a drink. I got there just in time to see Boris polishing off the veggie loaf in the dining room.

"No! **Bad dog. Bad dog!**" I whispered loudly.

Boris licked **his chops**. It was amazing he hadn't burned his mouth on the bubbling cheese.

How had Boris reached the dish? He wasn't exactly tall enough to reach the table.

"He used the stool," said a voice. I looked around. No one. The cloth on the dining table moved. I pulled it up to find Harry laying out his baseball cards on the floor.

"It **was pretty smart, actually**," said Harry. "Boris climbed onto the stool. Then he got up on the chair."

"Why didn't you stop him?"

Harry shrugged. Boris **waddled** under the table. He lay down, **with his head on Harry's knee.**

I heard footsteps from the kitchen. I pulled down the tablecloth and grabbed the empty dish. I wasn't sure what I was going to do with it. Mom walked in.

"David? **What did you do?**" she demanded.

If I told her the truth, Boris would get into trouble for eating the veggie loaf. Then I'd get in trouble for not putting him outside. There was no point in both of us getting in trouble.

"I ate it," I said. Then I licked the dish.

"You ate it?"

"I'm sorry. I was really hungry, Mom."

"What is everybody else supposed to have for dinner?" cried Mom. "Was there enough cheese?" she added.

"Yes."

"I added a little pesto. Could you taste it?"

"It was perfect, Mom," I said.

Mom smiled. Then she frowned when she remembered that she was mad at me.

"*Go to your room, David*," she said. "Wait till your father hears about this!"

In the next half hour I had some visitors.

First Dad came in and tried to frown.

"Your mother is **very upset**," he said loudly. "What did you really do with the veggie loaf?" he whispered.

I shrugged.

"Good idea," he said. "Don't tell me. **Your mother is furious**. And now I have to go out and get some **pizza**." He left humming.

Next came Zoe, who slapped my bedroom door.

"Good one, Dribbles."

Next came Harry, who shut the door quietly behind him.

"**You lied to Mom**," he said.

I shrugged.

"What's keeping me from telling her the truth?" he asked.

I stood up and leaned over him. He didn't seem too worried.

"Don't worry. I'll keep your secret," he said. "Either way you're in trouble."

After Harry left, Boris waddled into my room. He slumped onto the floor. His face looked very sad. His sides stuck out more than usual.

"Boris, what were you thinking?" I said.

Boris just burped. That's the problem with Boris. He doesn't think much at all.

Zoe came in after a few hours and handed me some **pizza**. She'd hidden it in her pencil case, so it was pretty squished, but I didn't care.

"Harry told me what happened," she said.

"Harry isn't good at keeping secrets," I said, before taking a bite.

"I hope **you** are," said Zoe.

Suddenly I wasn't hungry anymore.

"Have you talked to Mom and Dad yet?" I asked.

"Mom thought of a punishment for you. You're not going to like it," said Zoe, ignoring me.

"Have you told them?" I persisted.

"No. It's none of your business." Zoe zipped up her pencil case. "Just keep your mouth shut. Enjoy your dinner," she said as she left the room.

CHAPTER 6

THE SECRET MIXTURE

Mom came up with a **great plan to punish me.** I found out the next day after school. We'd had a substitute teacher, Miss Cochrane. **It had been a terrible day.**

I was in the middle of teaching Boris a trick when Mom walked into the living room.

"Mr. McCafferty called today," said Mom.

"I didn't do it," I said, waving a dog biscuit under Boris's nose.

"Actually, he called to get a gardener's phone number from me," said Mom. "Mr. McCafferty is getting his garden ready for the *Bays Park Fair* this weekend."

"That's nice," I said, waving the biscuit between Boris's eyes. **He sneezed an enormous sneeze. Slobber. Right in my face.**

"I told him to forget the handyman and that *you'd be there after school tomorrow to help*," said Mom.

"Okay," I said, wiping the Boris slobber off with my sleeve. "Wait. **What?**"

"It's either *help Mr. McCafferty, or be grounded for the weekend*," said Mom.

"But, Mom, Mr. McCafferty hates me. Hates! H-A-Y-T-E-S!" I yelled.

"There's no Y in hates," corrected Mom.

"I don't care. I'd rather be grounded for the weekend. Or my **whole life!**"

"Oh, David. Mr. McCafferty is just a *lonely old man* and I promised that you *would help him* in his garden. Besides, this weekend is the *Bays Park Fair*. You wouldn't want to miss out on that."

"**But, Mom!**"

I wanted to tell her that Mr. McCafferty **wasn't a nice, lonely, old man.** But the phone rang and Mom left the room. Something **wet and sloppy** slid across my hand. It was Boris's tongue.

"**It's all your fault!**" I said. Then I patted him. "You don't even know what you've done, do you, boy?"

Boris sneezed again, rolled over, and went to sleep.

* * *

"You're LATE," said Mr. McCafferty as he opened the door the next day.

It had been another long day without Ms. Stacey. I was getting worried.

"But I just got home."

"Well, come on. There's work to be done." Mr. McCafferty closed the door behind him.

I'd never been inside Mr. McCafferty's house. Joe and I had looked through the windows once. All we could see were stacks and stacks of newspapers. Most of the time the curtains were closed and you couldn't see in.

I wondered if Mr. McCafferty kept **dead bodies** in his house. Did he keep the newspapers for wrapping the bodies up? Maybe he was a **secret agent** for another country. Or some **kind of mad scientist!** That would fit in with him liking medical shows on TV.

Mr. McCafferty handed me some gardening gloves and a small shovel. "Gloves on. Then **wait here**," he said.

The gloves were too big. The extra parts at the end where my fingers didn't reach flopped around. **They smelled awful.**

Mr. McCafferty appeared, dragging a huge white bag. "We need to add some fertilizer to the soil."

"Fertilizer?" I asked.

"The secret to my success," he said, pointing at his huge roses. He waved me over to the bag, and then pushed my head deep into it. "**Smell that**," he said. "You won't get any fresher."

"That is disgusting!" I said. I pulled my head out of the bag. My eyes were **watering**. My stomach was doing some kind of skateboarding trick. Maybe **his fertilizer was the dead bodies of people all crunched up.**

"Excrement," said Mr. McCafferty. "My special recipe."

"**But it smells like poo!**" I yelled.

"**Exactly**," said Mr. McCafferty. "But not just any poo. It's a combination. I bet Mrs. Ching would love to find out what that combination is."

I nodded. Mrs. Ching was Mr. McCafferty's next-door neighbor. Each year they tried to **beat each other in the Best Rose competition** at the Bays Park Fair.

"You'll never guess the combination," said Mr. McCafferty. "Never." He laughed and patted his cat. "He'll never guess, will he, Mr. Figgins?"

I should have been sitting in front of the television with some cookies, a milkshake, and Boris. *I did not want to be with a weird old man and his horrible cat, talking about poo.* I knew fertilizer had something to do with farms. I thought about the kinds of animals that lived on farms.

"**Horse,**" I said.

Mr. McCafferty's smile started to fade. "Yes. Well, of course. That's easy to guess. What else?"

"**Cow,**" I said.

Mr. McCafferty's eyes narrowed. "Go on," he said.

I hummed "Old MacDonald Had a Farm" and thought about the words.

"That's cheating," said Mr. McCafferty.

"Chicken," I said.

"Yes," he agreed. "Well, that's all pretty easy to guess. But there's one **ingredient missing**. Would you like another smell?"

"No!" I said. I backed away.

The sound of **barking** caught my attention. The park was across from Mr. M.'s house. Someone had let a dog off its leash. The dog was chasing the ducks on the pond.

"**Duck!**" I said.

Mr. McCafferty grabbed my shoulder. **It was a pretty strong grip for a guy who was at least a hundred years old.** He leaned in close and whispered, "You've been **spying** on me, haven't you, boy?"

"No, Mr. McCafferty."

"Don't think I haven't seen you. You and your friends spying on me from the park. Well, this is a secret. Do you understand?"

"Yes sir."

"If Mrs. Ching ever finds out, I'll know who told her," he said.

"Not me, Mr. McCafferty."

"That's right. **I hear you're good at keeping secrets.** Let's hope that's true." He straightened up and grabbed the bag.

"But the fair is this weekend," I said. "How much good is this going to do?"

"It's all in the timing. That's part of the secret," he answered.

I wondered what was **hidden behind the closed curtains of Mr. M.'s house.** Suddenly I didn't want to **find out**.

CHAPTER 7

THE BAYS PARK FAIR

Ms. Stacey was at school the next day.

No one had admitted to changing her computer screensaver. Everyone in our class had to talk to Mr. Woods, one by one in the principal's office.

When it was my turn, Mr. Woods asked if I had touched Ms. Stacey's computer screensaver. **I said no.** He asked if I thought that I knew who did it. I said no. I didn't lie. I didn't think I knew who did it. **I knew exactly who did it.**

Mr. Woods said that was too bad. He said that starting Monday, our class was going to be **picking up garbage** every lunchtime until someone confessed.

Then Mr. Woods said that Ms. Stacey's mother had been sick. **Ms. Stacey had been sad.** We needed to help her and do the right thing.

I was sure the right thing would be to take Ms. Stacey to a **wrestling match**, but I didn't say that. Wrestling was a touchy subject at the moment.

Ms. Stacey seemed normal. She organized a **spelling quiz**. Then we had a **math test**. Then she gave us homework that needed to be in the next day, even though it would normally take us a whole week to complete.

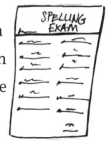

"Do you think she's still mad at us?" whispered Joe.

"No. I think she's happy to be back," I said.

"Really?" said Joe. He stared across the room. "I bet she's **still mad**."

"Until someone confesses, **none of us are off the hook**," I said.

"You're right," said Joe.

I thought about Victor. I couldn't tell Joe the truth.

"Now listen up, class," said Ms. Stacey. "The Bays Park Fair is this weekend. We need to make sure we're ready."

Every year, each class from Bays Park School did something at the fair. The theme for this year's fair was "**Going Green**." It was about **recycling**, composting, tree hugging and **stuff like that**. Harry's class was selling **green cotton candy**.

Our class had come up with a great idea. A **recycled minigolf course**. Each hole used recycled stuff. We had cans and boxes and cardboard tubes. There was wire and curtains and plastic drink bottles. Bec had done some awesome painting on material to make a **mini volcano**.

"There's a prize this year for the best entry," Ms. Stacey said. "Rose, do you think your mother could get **someone famous** to attend the fair?"

Great, I thought. We'd never hear the end of it. **Rose Thornton to the rescue.** Rose's mom had a special job working with lots of famous people. **Rose always talked about her mom's job.** Rose wouldn't have anything to talk about if it wasn't for that.

I looked at Rose. She sank in her seat.

"I'm not sure, Ms. Stacey," said Rose. "She's pretty busy these days."

What?

"Maybe I should call her?" Ms. Stacey suggested.

"No! Um, that's okay, Ms. Stacey. *I'll ask her myself.*"

"What's with her?" I asked Joe.

Joe was staring into space. Like he was thinking of eating a candy bar or a doughnut.

"Never mind," I said.

* * *

"What's up with Rose?" asked Bec at recess.

We'd just finished playing four square. Joe was still playing. I watched him flick the ball back to keep in the game.

"David?"

The next thing I knew, a rubber band hit my elbow.

"Ouch. What was that for?" I asked.

"I asked you a question. David, you're acting a little strange. Is something wrong?" Bec asked.

"I was just thinking about something else. Is that a crime?" I asked.

Getting married was a crime if you were Zoe's age, in this country, anyway. I couldn't stop thinking about my dumb sister and her dumb secret. I didn't want to keep her secret. In fact, **I didn't want to keep any secrets.**

"So what do you think? After school?" asked Bec.

"Uh, sure," I said.

"Great. We haven't had one in forever," said Bec.

"What?"

Then the bell rang and Bec ran inside. I followed her. I'd made a decision. If Zoe left the house, I was going to **follow her**. Maybe I'd find out who **her future husband** was. Maybe I could talk some sense into him. Since I had a plan, I felt a little better. That is, until Joe and Bec knocked on my door after school.

"I'm **busy** this afternoon," I said.

"But you said okay. And we haven't had a **Secret Club meeting** in forever," said Bec. "Someone else is here, too, just dying to see you," she added.

Ralph, Bec's pet rat, popped his head out of the front pouch of Bec's backpack.

I let them inside.

Loud music was pouring from under Zoe's bedroom door, so I figured she was still there. Joe said he was hungry. I made us some nachos. Then I heard the front door **slam**.

"**Oh no,**" I yelled. I looked out the window and saw Zoe walking down the road.

"I have to go," I shouted as I ran out the door.

"We're coming too," said Bec, grabbing her backpack.

"But I'm not done," said Joe, **shoving nachos in his mouth**.

Bec pushed Joe out the door after me.

"Okay, **time to spy**," I said. "Don't let her see us. Stay back. Keep quiet."

"Why are we **spying** on Zoe?" asked Joe.

"I can't tell you," I said. "**Will you still come?**"

They both nodded.

CHAPTER 8

SPYING

We walked past Mr. McCafferty's house. I saw the curtains TWITCH in his front room. While we were spying on Zoe, Mr. M. was spying on us. I guess he was still worried that I was going to tell his secret to Mrs. Ching. A gust of wind blew across from Mr. McCafferty's garden. It sent the awful smell of fertilizer up my nose.

"Yuck! What is that smell?" said Bec.

"Mr. McCafferty's roses," I said.

The roses looked **huge**. We passed Mrs. Ching's garden. I looked at her flowers. They seemed pretty big too.

"I saw you helping Mr. McCafferty with his garden, David." It was Mrs. Ching. She'd popped up out of nowhere. "That man needs all the help he can get. He thinks I don't know what he puts on his roses? I've watched him collect that duck poo from the pond."

Oh no! Mrs. Ching knew. Mr. M. was probably watching me talk to Mrs. Ching right now. If Mr. McCafferty ever found out she knew about the special ingredient, he'd think that I had told her! Then maybe I'd end up finding what Mr. McCafferty hid in his house. **Kids like me who couldn't keep a secret!**

"He's not as smart as he thinks he is," clucked Mrs. Ching. "There are *no secrets* in this neighborhood."

That's what you think, I thought.

"Yes, Mrs. Ching," I said. I rushed ahead and caught up with my friends.

Zoe walked quickly. She never once looked back. The streets got **narrower** and the buildings got **taller**. Then Zoe disappeared up an alley. I put my hand in the air to tell the others to stop. I counted to sixty. Then I peeked around the corner just in time to hear a door SLAM.

"Great!" I said.

"**Where'd she go?**" asked Joe.

"**I don't know,**" I answered.

"What stores are here?" Bec asked.

I looked up the alley. "**Accountant?**" said Joe, reading one of the signs.

I shook my head.

"Hair stylist?" asked Bec.

"Maybe," I said.

"Dyson's Employment Agency?" said Bec.

I shook my head.

"Weddings by Shannel? Organic Food?" said Bec.

"What did you say?" I asked.

"Organic Food?" repeated Bec.

"No. **Before that.**"

"Weddings by Shannel?"

"Hey look! Isn't that Rose and her mom?" said Joe.

"There's Zoe," said Bec, grabbing my arm.

I ignored the Thorntons and concentrated on my sister. She had left Weddings by Shannel and was walking back up the alley towards us.

"Quick," I said. "Let's get out of here."

We hid just in time behind a large van. Ralph, thinking it was a game, crawled out of Bec's bag and ran off.

"No, Ralphy!" whispered Bec.

I slid out from behind the van and looked around for Ralph. He'd found the hugest garbage can. It looked like he might want to live there. I grabbed him. He gave a little squeak, just as Rose and her mom walked past. I ducked behind the can. I was pretty sure they didn't see me.

After about five minutes, Joe let out a huge sigh of relief from behind the van.

"Okay, David," said Bec. "What's going on?"

"I can't tell you," I said.

"Is it Rose Thornton?" asked Joe.

I shook my head.

"Is it about Ms. Stacey's computer?" asked Bec.

"I can't tell you," I said.

"**Wow**!" said Joe. "I never thought you were the **Screensaver Intruder**."

"I'm not," I snapped.

"But you know **who** is?" asked Bec.

"I can't say," I said.

"What did Jake Davern want to tell you the other day?" asked Bec.

"I can't say," I said.

"And that girl," said Joe. "What was that all about?"

I shook my head.

"And Victor Sneddon? You **NEVER** told us what he said," said Joe.

"**I can't**," I said.

"I know, I know," said Bec. "You can't say." She put her hands on her hips. "You're not saying a lot lately, David. **Friends tell each other stuff. Are we friends or not?**"

I felt trapped. "Look, it's a **secret**. They're all secrets. You're not supposed to tell secrets, are you?" I thought about Dad's proud face when he found out I'd kept Smorgan's secret. "Joe, if you told me a secret, would you want me telling everyone?"

"I guess not," he said.

"Bec?"

She shook her head.

"Okay. People have told me **secrets**. I didn't ask them to. But I have to deal with it myself."

For once, Bec had NOTHING to say.

* * *

After dinner I got a call from Rose.

"What are you doing **spying** on me?" she asked. "And don't try to deny it, because I *saw you.*"

"I wasn't spying on you."

"You think you're so clever, David Baxter. You don't care if you ruin other people's lives. Well, *my mother didn't get fired*, if that's what you're thinking. *She just decided she didn't want to work in PR anymore.*"

"Is this a secret?" I asked weakly.

"Yes. Now you have to keep it. Until I tell you to. And I'm NEVER going to talk to you **again**!" Then I heard a dial tone.

So, while Zoe had been looking at the white dresses in the bridal shop, Mrs. Thornton had been looking for a new job at Dyson's Employment Agency. That was bad timing.

The phone rang again. I picked it up.

"I thought you weren't going to talk to me again," I said.

"What? Hello, Davey." It was Smashing Smorgan.

Smorgan wanted to tell me about his photo shoot for the **Hall of Fame**.

"Of course, I had to organize it myself," he complained. "I didn't realize how much work Ivan did."

"Who's Ivan?" I asked.

"My old manager. I'm looking for a new one, Davey. Just keep it in mind," he said.

That night I couldn't get to SLEEP. I tried counting sheep, but that just reminded me of Mr. M.'s special **fertilizer**. I tried reciting the alphabet backward, but that just reminded me of Mrs. Cochrane, our substitute teacher. I couldn't help thinking that if I hadn't known a famous person like Smorgan, I would never be in this mess.

Finally, I decided to make a list. That's what my dad does when he has too many things to think about. I got up and switched on my bed lamp. I reached under my bed to a secret spot and grabbed my diary.

Secrets

Smashing Smorgan screensaver — VS, not on purpose

Jake D — Delete story, mistake

K L J

Boris — VL eat (will Harry keep?)

Mr. M magic d. poo

Mr. M magic d. poo

Mrs. T no j

Zoe — happy ever after?

Once I'd written down all the stuff going around in my head, I felt much better. I marked the list with the diary's ribbon bookmark. I turned off my light. Then I had a **crazy nightmare** where Zoe 𝕄𝔸ℝℝ𝕀𝔼𝔻 Mr. McCafferty. The bridesmaids **were ducks** and Mrs. Thornton's **new job was playing the wedding music**.

It wasn't until the weekend that I realized I hadn't put my diary back in **its secret spot**.

CHAPTER 9

The Friday before the **Bays Park Fair**, Joe wasn't at school.

"Mrs. Pagnopolous said JOE had a cold," explained Bec.

"That's too bad," said Ms. Stacey.

During Math, someone slipped me an **envelope**. The word "Joe" was written on the front in a girl's writing. Each letter was a different color.

"Could you give this to Joe, David? Just tell him I hope he gets better soon."

I looked up and recognized Kaya, one of Rose's friends. She had **long black hair** and really white teeth. She could have been in a toothpaste ad. This was the girl whose story Jake Davern had lost on the computer. This was the girl who thought Joe was cool.

I grabbed my math book, my pens, and the note and sat next to Bec. She wasn't surprised about the note. It turned out that Bec already knew that Joe liked Kaya right back.

I told Bec that someone had told me that Kaya liked Joe, but I had to keep it a secret. Bec laughed. "She wanted you to tell him," said Bec.

"She did?"

"Sure. When someone tells you that someone else really likes your friend, then it's **okay** for you to tell your friend that someone likes them. You need to tell Joe that Kaya likes him. That will make him happy."

"Okay," I said.

I wondered if Bec could help me with my other secrets. If I didn't use any names, maybe it would be all right to tell her.

"Bec, what if someone — let's call him V — did something to someone else's computer and you knew about it but it was a secret?"

"David, if you know it's Victor, you have to tell a teacher," Bec said, shaking her head.

Then Ms. Stacey rang the tiny brass bell on her desk. It was the end of Math. I went back to my desk.

It was time to talk about the fair.

Everyone in our class had a task. There was a list. That was so people could work on the mini-golf course for a while. Then they could go and look at the rest of the fair. Jake Davern kept telling everyone that he would be onstage in the Performance Tent. He wouldn't tell us what he was doing. I guessed it had something to do with **monkeys**. Ms. Stacey asked Rose whether her mother had arranged a **special guest** for the day.

"Could I talk to you after class?" said Rose.

Rose was going to have to tell the truth.

Then I had an idea. When I got home I'd make a couple of calls that could make TWO **people** very happy.

* * *

I managed to make it home without Bec **bugging** me about **turning Victor over** to the teachers.

I wondered what was worse. Twenty-two **angry** people in my class? Or one huge Victor Sneddon?

I made my phone calls. Then Mr. McCafferty called. He told me he'd seen me talking to Mrs. Ching.

"She talked to me, Mr. McCafferty. It wasn't my fault," I said.

"We'll see," he said. "You'd better hope she doesn't win a blue *ribbon this year.*"

* * *

In the morning, Dad knocked on my door. "Rise and shine! Breakfast is ready. It's a beautiful day for the fair," he said.

Dad loved the **Bays Park Fair**. Every year he got the events list. Then he would circle the things that we couldn't miss. This year there were more circles than usual.

Dad, Harry, and I sat at the table eating breakfast. Mom kept running in and out, muttering. Zoe was nowhere to be seen.

"We will leave the house at 10 a.m. sharp," said Dad, checking the brochure. "David needs to be at the **mini-golf course at 10:30** a.m. That leaves us enough time to find a parking spot."

"Check!" said Harry.

"At exactly **11:15** a.m. Harry will start his shift at the cotton candy stand. Then at **12:30** we will all meet at the Common for lunch. At **1:15** we will make our way to the Home Produce Hall, where the announcement for the baking entries will be made."

"What are we going there for?" I asked.

"Your mother's entering her **vegetarian loaf**," said Dad, keeping a straight face. "Then Zoe will start **her shift at the Performance Tent at 1:30 p.m.**"

"And we can do what we want," said Harry.

"And the rest of the family will proceed to the Flower Judging Competition to **show support for Mr. McCafferty**. After that, we will move to the Performance Tent to watch Zoe perform **whatever it is she's performing**."

"Do I have to go to the Flower Competition?" I asked. I didn't want to be around when Mrs. Ching won the Best Rose in Show.

There was heavy thudding coming from the front door. Like we were going to be invaded by an army or something.

"Gran's here," squealed Harry. He ran to the door.

Worse than an army, I thought.

"I've been waiting out here for *half an hour*," said Gran angrily, as she pushed past Harry. "I need a cup of tea. *Have you been keeping out of trouble, David?*"

The fun just never stopped at my house.

CHAPTER 10

A SURPRISE WIN

It was a **typical Baxter day**. Dad stood around pointing at his watch, but not actually doing anything. Mom rushed from one room to another. Gran wanted to talk to me, but I tried to stay out of her way. Zoe stayed in bed for as long as possible. **She was probably trying to decide what her bridesmaids would wear.** Harry just got in the way.

Just when I thought it would never happen, we all piled into the cars. We had to take two cars, because there were six of us. Gran insisted on driving **her shiny new sports car**, which only seemed to go five miles an hour.

We got to the fair **five minutes ahead** of Dad's schedule.

I got to the Recycled Mini-golf Course on time and started handing out balls and putters. **Joe**, who was **wearing a huge scarf** around his neck, was collecting the balls.

Bec was out front SHOUTING for people to come and play. Ralph was sitting on her shoulder. Kaya kept walking past with some of the GG's, giggling.

I finally handed the note to Joe. "Joe, this is from Kaya. She thinks you're really cool," I said.

"She does?" said Joe. His eyes looked like they might **pop out** of his head.

"Yeah. It's a secret. But I thought you should know," I said.

"Okay," said Joe. Then he went to collect more balls. He had a HUGE smile on his face.

Ms. Stacey was taking the money for each round of golf. She seemed pretty happy. I wanted to tell her about Victor. Every time I thought about doing it, my insides melted like jelly. It didn't seem fair that a whole class would have to pay for someone else's mistake.

I walked over backwards to her so I couldn't see her getting closer and I couldn't chicken out. I finally **bumped** into her.

"Oh. Hi, Ms. Stacey," I said.

"Hi David," she said.

"This is great, isn't it?"

"It's going very well," she said. She shook her coin box.

"How's your mother, Ms. Stacey?"

"She's much better. Thank you for asking," she said with a smile.

"About your screensaver," I began.

Ms. Stacey raised her eyebrows. "Yes?" she asked.

I took a breath and told her about Victor's secret.

"Well, thank you for telling me, David. I think you're very brave. Sometimes secrets that hurt other people need to be told."

"Victor is definitely going to hurt me when he finds out I told you," I said.

"Actually, Victor told me this morning. He was helping me set up the golf course and he just blurted it out," said Ms. Stacey.

"He did?"

"So you're *off the hook*," said Ms. Stacey. "But you did the *right thing*."

That's when I decided I'd tell Mom and Dad about **Zoe getting married**. I figured I'd wait until we got home that night.

Joe ran over. "Ms. Stacey, Ms. Stacey. Look!" He pointed into the crowd that had gathered outside our golf course. Mrs. Thornton and Rose were leading **three huge green monsters** our way. It was Smashing Smorgan and two of his friends, skin painted green and in their **wrestling outfits**, snarling and snapping.

I looked at Ms. Stacey, who suddenly looked green herself.

"Hi, *Lisa*," said Mrs. Thornton. I realized she was talking to Ms. Stacey. **Ms. Stacey had a first name!**

"They're green," said Ms. Stacey weakly.

"For the fair's green theme," said Mrs. Thornton. "I've decided to open my own PR agency. *Thanks to David, Smorgan is my first client*," she said proudly.

My idea had worked! I looked at Rose, but she just scowled at me.

Then Dad came by. He pointed to his watch. "It's 12:25, David. **Time for lunch**," he said. Joe and Bec had also finished their shifts. Dad invited them to join us.

Before we left, a fair official slapped a **Best Show Entry blue ribbon** on our mini-golf sign. Dad and I agreed that we probably would have won without the **three green wrestler celebrities**. I thought it was cool anyway.

The whole family sat down on a blanket to eat lunch. Mom pulled out box after box of food. As usual, she had made enough for twenty people. Bec fed Ralph some crumbs from her sandwich. Joe took off his scarf. For once, Gran wasn't picking on me. She was leaning against a tree with her eyes closed.

Zoe suddenly stood up. "Oh **no!**" she wailed. "I forgot **my performance piece**."

"Can't you **just remember it?**" said Harry. His hair looked green after his shift at the cotton candy stall.

"I'll never remember it," said Zoe. "I spent forever on it. NOW I'll miss out."

"Where is it?" asked Mom.

"In my bedside drawer," said Zoe. "I wrote it in my diary."

"I'll get it," said Gran, her eyes still closed.

"No, Mom, I'll go," said Dad.

"Don't be silly, Thomas. I drove here, didn't I? I am capable of going back to get the diary by myself. I gave it to her. I know what it looks like. Isn't it time for the Home Produce Hall?"

Mom screamed. Everyone started packing up the picnic things. Zoe hugged Gran. That was something she hadn't done in years. Then we all rushed off to the Hall.

"Maybe I should **have gone with her**," said Dad as we sat in front of the Produce stage.

"She'll be fine," said Mom.

Then we had to be quiet. The presenter talked about the **quality of entries**.

Then he gave some awards. Bec was playing silent **peek-a-boo** with Ralph, who was popping in and out of her pocket. Finally we got to the Vegetarian Section.

"And the winner of the **vegetarian section**," said the presenter, "for her interesting take on Mediterranean cuisine, and in keeping with our **green theme**, is Cordelia Baxter."

Everyone clapped. Except for the Baxter family, of course. We were in shock. Luckily Mom didn't notice. She RAN to the stage.

"Congratulations, Mrs. Baxter. What inspired you to create 'Mediterranean Loaf'?"

The announcer handed Mom the microphone. "Well," she said loudly. "I always like to experiment with my recipes. Just this week I tried something new. My son liked it so much he polished off the whole loaf."

"Looks like veggie loaf will be a **family favorite** in the Baxter household for **many years to come**," said the announcer.

CHAPTER 11

ONSTAGE

After Mom won, Zoe left for her shift at the Performance Tent. The rest of us went straight to the **Flower Exhibition.**

The Flower Exhibition was in a huge greenhouse. There were lots of different plants, flowers in jars, and flowers in pots. It was **really boring.**

"Look for Mr. *McCafferty's roses,*" said Mom. "They should be in the Best Rose in Show category."

Mr. McCafferty appeared from out of nowhere and glared at me. **He looked like he was trying to figure out how many sheets of newspaper he'd need to wrap my dead body in.**

"Baxter family," he said, nodding at us.

"How did you do, Mr. McCafferty?" asked Dad.

"**Second prize,**" barked Mr. McCafferty.

Uh-oh! Mrs. Ching had won and I was dead.

"That's great," said Mom. "And *Mrs. Ching?*"

"We **tied**," said Mr. McCafferty. "Someone new, Fay Anthony from Lorimer Street, has won first prize."

"Well, second prize is nothing to SNEEZE at," said Mom.

Joe sneezed. Then he put his scarf back on. Mr. McCafferty glared at Joe.

The adults talked a little more. I was so glad Mr. McCafferty was mad at Fay Anthony, and not at me.

Then we went to the rides. I went on the Regurgitator and The Flame, which shot out real fire flames when the ride got going. Harry and Bec were the only ones who went on **The Drop Zone**. It was a huge ride that dropped thousands of feet out of the sky to the ground. The ride was over in three seconds. Joe and I agreed that it was a dumb ride.

Then Dad hurried us off to the Performance Tent. We were a little early, but Gran was already there.

"Did you get the diary?" asked Mom.

"Of course," said Gran.

We settled into our seats. Joe sat next to Kaya.

"OOOOOH," said the GG's.

The announcer said, "The next item on our program is Jake Davern. Jake will present a poem, 'A Green Sorry'."

The audience clapped politely.

Poetry? Jake Davern? It was probably something about green monkeys.

Jake appeared from behind the curtains. He coughed.

"'A Green Sorry,'" he said. Then he continued:

"I'm feeling quite green

I'm feeling very mean

I just want to say

On story writing day

When you had a story

That you'd forgotten to worry

To save and not delete

You left to have a treat

But I didn't know

And I gave you lots of woe

By turning off the hard drive

Your story — no more alive

Was gone

Like a song

On a turned-off radio

Hey-de-ho

Sorry."

Then he bowed.

The crowd **clapped loudly**. It just goes to show you, I thought. **People can surprise** you sometimes.

"Thank you very much, Jake," said the announcer.

Jake grinned and walked off the stage.

"And next on our program is **Zoe Baxter** with her piece, '**A Modern–day Love Story**.' Zoe describes it as Romeo and Juliet revisited, in keeping with our recycled theme."

Zoe appeared at the microphone without her diary.

"Um, does someone have my diary? Gran?" said Zoe, looking out into the audience.

"Oh!" said Gran. She pulled the diary out from her bag. "Hurry, David."

I ran to the stage. Zoe grabbed the diary from me.

"'A Modern-day Love Story,'" announced Zoe.

I stood at the side of the stage to watch her. She opened up the book at the ribbon bookmark. Then she coughed and looked at me.

"Go ahead," whispered someone from behind the curtain.

"Secrets," said Zoe. Then she continued:

"Smashing Smorgan screensaver — VS, not on purpose

Jake D — Delete story, mistake

K L J

Boris — VS eat (will Harry keep?)

Mr. M magic d. poo

Mrs. T no j

Zoe — happy-ever-after?"

Then she stopped. I started clapping loudly. Zoe bowed and walked offstage. The rest of the audience joined in the clapping. **No one seemed to realize that an entire list of secrets I was supposed to keep had just been announced to the whole world.** As a keeper of secrets, I was a FAILURE.

Gran stayed for dinner. So did Bec and Joe. I was staying out of Zoe's way. If she was mad at me now, she'd really be mad when I **blabbed** her secret to Mom and Dad.

"How did David's diary get into my bedside drawer?" complained Zoe.

"I found a diary in the laundry the other day," said Mom. "I thought it was yours, Zoe, so I put it back into your drawer."

"I wasted hours writing my piece for nothing," said Zoe.

"Why don't you **read it to us**?" suggested Dad.

"It's too late now," said Zoe.

"I'll get it," said Harry. He ran to Zoe's room.

"Manners!" said Gran. "Really, Thomas. Are we having dinner, or listening to a performance?"

"We're doing both, Mother," said Dad.

I was trying to get up the courage to mention Zoe's wedding. There just didn't seem to be a right time. But Mom and Dad would be really hurt if Zoe went off and got married without her telling them.

"Speaking of weddings," I said finally.

"No, we weren't," said Gran.

"Mom. Dad. There's something I have to tell you. I was hoping Zoe would tell you. It's her secret. But this has gone on too long."

I took a breath. "Zoe's going to be wearing white real soon," I said.

"What?" said Dad.

"That will make a nice change," said Gran.

"She's going to be walking down the aisle. With flowers. And music and rings and stuff."

"**Dribbles**, what are you talking about?" said Zoe.

"Don't deny it, Zoe! You're getting married."

CHAPTER 12

NO MORE SECRETS

The whole dining table erupted like the crowd at a **wrestling match**. People were **talking, gasping, yelling, and crying**. Even Boris started howling. Harry walked in. **He handed the diary to Zoe.**

Zoe stood and opened the diary. She started reading out her performance piece. The room fell silent. Then she got to " . . . but I love him. If our parents don't agree, we'll just have to run away and get married. It's the only way I can survive."

Hmmm. **That sounded familiar.**

Joe clapped, then stopped when Bec nudged him.

"Is this what you read the other day, David?" asked Zoe.

I nodded.

"Did you think I was going to run off and get married?" she asked.

"I thought that was **the secret I had to keep**," I said.

"David, I am 15! I think I'm old enough not to do something as stupid as that!" said Zoe.

"But if that's not the secret, why did you go to Weddings by Shannel the other day?" I asked.

"How do you know that?" asked Zoe. "Have you been **spying** on me, you little brat?"

"What's this about?" asked Mom.

"I got a job. For the summer. If you'll let me. It doesn't pay much, but I'd get to learn a lot."

"I don't have a problem with that," said Dad. "So why the **secret?**"

Zoe opened her diary again. She flipped to a new section. Then she read:

"I haven't got all the information yet. I want to have all the facts. Mom and Dad have talked about me doing science. About maybe going into research, like Dad. I do like math and science. But I'd rather be a clothes designer. I just don't know how to tell them."

So that was Zoe's **real secret.**

"**Oh**," said Dad.

"See, I knew you'd be mad," said Zoe.

"**I'm not mad**," said Dad. "I am glad you're not getting married, though. Let's talk about this later. Maybe your mother and I can have a meeting with you and your school career advisor."

"Really?" said Zoe. "You'd let me be a clothes designer?"

"I hope you're not only going to design black clothes," said Gran. "I won't buy any of them. Now, is there dessert? Or do I have to get up and make something myself?"

Suddenly I felt light. Like I was a **helium balloon** and I would float away into the sky if somebody didn't tie me down. My sister wasn't running off to get married. I didn't have any more secrets.

I NEVER wanted to keep another secret.

"I made dessert," said Mom, getting up. "Harry, help clear the table, please."

Mom had a big smile on her face.

"You'll all be happy to know I've decided to enter next year's dessert section at the fair," Mom said. "I've created a new recipe. I call it **Bombe Bays Park**."

"What?" said Gran. "Did she say *she was going to bomb Bays Park?*"

"It's a dessert," Bec explained.

"Desert? Don't be ridiculous, child. Bays Park isn't a desert," said Gran.

Everyone OOHED and AHHED when Mom came out with a flaming mound of dessert.

It wasn't Boris's fault that he was sleeping in the **wrong spot**.

Mom tripped over him and the dessert ended up on the table, where it set fire to the tablecloth.

Then the smoke alarm went off.

Everyone rushed around, except Ralph and Gran and Dad and me. Ralph just looked at the dessert crumbs on the table. Gran kept talking about the desert. Dad put his arm around my shoulder as we watched the madness.

"Now, **there's** the secret to a ᕼᗩᑭᑭᖴ family," he said. Mom was slapping at the flaming tablecloth with her napkin. Then the napkin caught on fire.

"A secret? Dad, I am never to going to keep another secret again," I said. "Ever."

"That's okay, David. Feel **free** to tell everyone."

"So what's the secret?" I asked.

"**Togetherness**," said Dad.

The End

About the Author

When Karen Tayleur was growing up, her father told her many stories about his own childhood. These stories continued to grow. She says, "I always enjoyed the retelling, and wanted to create a character who had the same abilities with 'bending the truth.'" And David Mortimore Baxter was born! Karen lives in Australia with her husband, two children, two cats, and one dog.

About the Illustrator

Brann Garvey grew up in the great state of Iowa, where he studied art and visual communications. He graduated from the Minneapolis College of Art & Design with a degree in illustration. Brann is usually found with one or more of the following: a pencil in his hand, a comic book, a remote for watching DVDs, or his pet kitty, Iggy. When the weather is nice, Brann likes to play disc golf, and he proudly points out that Iowa is one of the world's centers for the sport. Iggy does not play.

Glossary

composting (KOM-pohst-ing)—fertilizing with a mixture of decaying organic matter, such as leaves and manure

confess (kuhn-FESS)—to say that something is true

delete (di-LEET)—to remove

fame (FAYM)—the quality of being very well known

guilty (GIL-tee)—having committed a crime or offense; feeling shame

ingredient (in-GREE-dee-uhnt)—a separate part of a mixture

intruder (in-TROO-dur)—one who breaks in a house; or interferes or meddles

ransom (RAN-suhm)—a price paid to rescue or save someone, or have someone set free

rumor (ROO-mur)—something said by people that may or may not be true

villain (VIL-uhn)—someone who is wicked or evil

wrestler (RESS-lur)—someone who fights by grasping and tripping or throwing an opponent

Discussion Questions

1. Can you keep a secret? How do you decide if and when you should tell a secret? Why and when do you ask others to keep secrets for you?

2. On page 5, David feels that when Smashing Smorgan told him a secret, "it was a bad time to have Smorgan as a friend." Why did he feel this way? Did David feel the same way about Smorgan and telling secrets by the end of the book? Explain your answers.

3. Why did the other characters in the book start telling David their secrets?

4. "Sometimes secrets that hurt other people need to be told." Do you agree or disagree with this statement? Explain.

Writing Prompts

1. At the end of the book, David's dad says that the secret to a happy family is togetherness. Write about what you think is the secret to a happy family. Explain your thoughts.

2. Bec says that "friends tell each other stuff." Do you agree or disagree with her? Explain your answer.

3. What makes people "famous?" Write about someone you consider to be famous and what makes him/her so.

4. Do you keep a diary? What's in it? How would you feel if someone else read it? Explain.

David Mortimore Baxter

David is a great kid, but he has one big problem—he can't stop talking. These wildly humorous stories, told by David himself, will show readers just how much trouble a boy and his mouth can get into, whether he's making promises to become class president or bragging that he's best friends with the world's most famous wrestler. David is amiable, engaging, cool, and smart enough to realize that growing up is the biggest adventure of all.

Internet Sites

Do you want to know more about subjects related to this book? Or are you interested in learning about other topics? Then check out FactHound, a fun, easy way to find Internet sites.

Our investigative staff has already sniffed out great sites for you!

Here's how to use FactHound:

1. Visit *www.facthound.com*

2. Select your grade level.

3. To learn more about subjects related to this book, type in the book's ISBN number: **1598890778**.

4. Click the **Fetch It** button.

FactHound will fetch the best Internet sites for you!